SPECIAL COLLECTOR'S EDITION

Disney's TARZAN ®

Storyboard drawing by Glen Keane.

Russell Schroeder & Victoria Saxon

Illustrated with artwork created by

Walt Disney Feature Animation

Disney PRESS

We would like to thank Bonnie Arnold,
Danton Burroughs, Howard Green, Eric Daniels,
Kevin Lima, Juliet Nees, and Janet and Beryl Mann
for their assistance in preparing this book.

**Character study
by Mike Surrey.**

First Edition
1 3 5 7 9 10 8 6 4 2

This book is set in 12-point Journal Text.
Book design by Edward Miller.

Library of Congress Catalog Card Number: 99–60400
ISBN 0-7868-3221-5 (trade)—ISBN 0-7868-5093-0 (lib. bdg.)
For more Disney Press fun, visit www.DisneyBooks.com

Storyboard drawing by Glen Keane.

CONTENTS

Visual development art by Vance Gerry.

**Character study
by Glen Keane.**

THE EXPEDITION IS PROPOSED

eginning production of an animated feature is like starting out on a grand adventure. It's a journey that, once begun, will take many years to complete. It requires hardy companions who possess a spirit of teamwork and who are equally dedicated to facing challenges and overcoming obstacles. It relies on the daily supplies that will sustain the expedition. It can even inspire the creation of special tools that will enable the adventurers to march into territory never before explored. And it's a journey filled with surprises and rewards.

Of course, someone must suggest that the expedition begin. One day, the proposal was made at Walt Disney Feature Animation, "Why don't we use Edgar Rice Burroughs's Tarzan character as the subject of an animated feature?"

That suggestion was met with an almost unanimous response: "Why?" After all, *Tarzan* is the second-most-filmed literary property in the world. The adventures of the ape-man have become a familiar part of popular culture. What more could Disney bring to this story?

There was a ready answer to that skeptical, although understandable, *why*. The Disney animators could explore and fully develop a part of Tarzan's life that most films have ignored: Tarzan's very special relationship with the ape family that took him in, particularly the bond that was established between him and his adoptive mother, the gorilla Kala.

When this very important part of the story was considered, it was clear that here was an approach to the tale that fell directly into the area of Disney's expertise. Making talking animals believable personalities that an audience could relate to and root for has been a tradition at the Studio since its earliest days.

Visual development art by Paul Felix.

Visual development art by H. B. Lewis shows young Tarzan's close relationship with his ape mother, Kala.

What wasn't immediately expected, however, was the unique approach to the character of Tarzan himself that would be taken by supervising animator Glen Keane and his team. What they envisioned and eventually achieved would set Disney's characterization of Tarzan apart from all his previous film incarnations. And it would provide the uncontestable answer: This is why the hero of Edgar Rice Burroughs's classic tales is the perfect subject for an adventure in animated filmmaking.

An early drawing by visual development artist Paul Felix reflects a more traditional approach to Tarzan's vine swinging.

When supervising animator Glen Keane joined the production, his initial rough drawings captured Tarzan's animal-like energy.

A SCOUTING TRIP:
AFRICAN SAFARI

It has become a tradition at Walt Disney Feature Animation that once a story idea is decided upon, a trip to that story's locale is undertaken. This is so that a key group of the film's creative personnel can become inspired by the actual setting and share their discoveries with their colleagues back home in a way that can only result from having actually been there.

Directors Kevin Lima and Chris Buck, art director Dan St. Pierre, head of story Brian Pimental, David Stainton, Doug Ball, and Paul Felix all set out on a two-week trek through Africa.

For Dan St. Pierre, being in the forest verified his belief that the film should capture the strength and depth of the jungle.

A local warning sign doesn't appear to dampen the high spirits of the Disney visitors.

The Bwindi Forest is a place where nature totally surrounds and dominates the visitor.

As conceived by the Disney artists, Tarzan's jungle would become an overwhelming, sheltering, and bountiful home for its inhabitants, almost a character in itself. Visual development art of Gorilla Valley by Paul Felix.

Even the African sunsets contributed inspiration. Kevin Lima and Chris Buck are bathed in the hot red glow of a brilliant evening—a dramatic tone that appears in several scenes in the movie, adding to a sequence's emotional impact.

As well as deriving inspiration from the jungle's lush plant life, the Disney visitors happened upon many of the animal residents, who would also play a part in the final film.

In Masai Mara, a real-life Sabor prowls the trees above the visitors.

The red soil used by the elephants for their dust baths transformed their normal gray hide into a color that inspired the animation palette. Thus we see Tarzan's pal Tantor as an attractive reddish brown pachyderm who enlivens the scenes he is in with his color as much as his personality.

Visiting the Sweetwater Chimp Sanctuary, Kevin Lima discovered the wonder of bonding with these cousins of Tarzan's gorilla family. "All in all, this was one of the great experiences of my life."

Young Oliver Smith and his chimpanzee companion were obviously buddies who shared a mutual curiosity.

And they tussled playfully, much in the way being devised for Tarzan and his pal Terk.

Probably the most eagerly anticipated part of the trip was the chance to see gorillas up close. It takes a keen observer to locate these powerful, but normally shy and gentle creatures, for they are often deep within foliage, barely visible.

Coming within eight feet of one gorilla, the experience was, according to Chris Buck, "awe-inspiring, a dream come true."

When it came time for portraying the apes in the movie, the Disney visitors remembered what they had observed. Tarzan's gorilla family is often seen within the shadows of protective covering.

BASE CAMP
WALT DISNEY FEATURE ANIMATION, BURBANK, CALIFORNIA

When the members of the African expedition returned to their home facility in Burbank, they found a growing staff of companions who would join them in the four-year journey of creating Walt Disney Feature Animation's version of the *Tarzan* story. Eventually numbering several hundred men and women, the crew would consist of artists, technicians, supervisors, support personnel, musicians, actors, and others, all dedicated to the task of taking a popular literary classic and transforming it into a unique film experience.

Background painting by Philip Philipson

EXPEDITION GUIDES

Every expedition relies on those people who oversee all the journey's requirements, make sure everything is where it should be when needed, and support the members of their expedition in the tasks that face them. With their encouragement and guidance, they help each person in the party conquer new challenges, explore new territory, and ascend formidable heights.

The primary guides for Disney's *Tarzan* were the directors, Kevin Lima and Chris Buck, who shared the overall vision of what the film is to be; art director Dan St. Pierre and associate art director Dan Cooper, who worked with color and form to shape the story and characters in the appropriately dramatic way; and the producer, Bonnie Arnold, who helped define goals, smoothed bumpy paths, and provided creative sustenance.

Tarzan leads the human visitors to the gorilla nesting area, much in the way the film's producer and directors accompany the various creative teams through the tangles and shadows of the filmmaking process and help lead them toward the brightness of the final goal: a completed movie.

Color Key painting by Joachim Royo Morales from a workbook sketch by Fred Craig.

EXPLORING THE TERRAIN

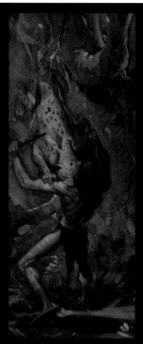

Basing their concepts on *Tarzan of the Apes*, the very first book in Edgar Rice Burroughs's series, a group of visual development artists began producing artwork that presented the dramatic events of the story. The artwork portrayed the relationships between Tarzan and his ape family and devised the jungle setting that would serve as a backdrop for the fantastic adventure.

John Watkiss produced over eighty paintings that covered the events of the original story.

Cinematic in format, the paintings are filled with a dynamic tension. Even in a study where the characters are at rest, one gets the feeling that they will explode into action at any second.

Many artists looked at the ways Tarzan and the apes might relate to each other. Whether they examined Tarzan's earliest introduction to the ape family, as in this illustration by Brian Pimental . . .

. . . presented this studied conversation . . .

. . . looked at an exchange of heated words . . .

. . . or just captured a playful moment, Tarzan's life among the apes was depicted as full and varied as that of any family group.

All other art on this page by Paul Felix.

17

Each character in the film is defined by shape, attitude, expression, and, in the case of the human characters, by costume. The artists in charge of visual development explore the paths that will lead them to establishing a unique personality for each character that is compatible with the overall story line and art direction.

Above: **Paul Felix dramatizes Jane's rescue from the angry baboons.**
Left: **An early concept of Tantor and Terk by H. B. Lewis contrasts the large elephant's affectionate nature with Terk's very unsentimental personality.**

Rick Maki shows how Professor Porter might engage in data gathering.

Staging story ideas and capturing various moods all fall within the visual development artist's realm, helping to inspire and build the story line and settings for the film.

During the visual development process, no story idea is too bizarre, for at this stage anything is possible; everything is worth considering and may spark additional creativity.

Below: **The elephant herd provides Tarzan with a graceful underwater performance worthy of *Fantasia*. Painting by Nick Domingo from a drawing by Paul Felix.**

Artists also looked at the ways Tarzan's jungle home should appear.
Some early paintings were basically realistic representations of the African
jungle. Some, such as this example, made it look exotically idealized.

Visual development art by Bryan Jowers.

What was finally chosen was a jungle that looks as if it has grown and
thrived for centuries, never having been disturbed by man until the
events of the film's story.

It was also decided to give a distinct look to the living areas chosen
by the story's characters.

Gorillas prefer to stay in sheltered, protective areas, so Tarzan's family chooses lushly dense parts of the jungle, away from full, direct sunlight. Background painting by Theirry Fournier.

The human visitors, Professor Porter, his daughter Jane, and their guide, Clayton, feel safe in bright, open areas. They set up their camp in a clearing, surrounded by tall, straight bamboo that, because of its vertical, almost architectural appearance, makes one think of the buildings in their cities back home. Background painting by Don Moore.

The home Tarzan's parents make for themselves after their shipwreck combines elements from what the humans are comfortable with and what the gorillas prefer. Built with wreckage from the ship, their house is architectural and man-made. But that house is built in a tall, supporting tree, in which the natural curves are like those found in Gorilla Valley.

Layout drawing of the tree house by Ian Gooding.

Color visual development art of tree house by Ian Gooding.

22

The art directors carefully created the design and color of a setting to underscore the scene's emotions.

To reflect Jane's distress during the baboon chase, the gentle curves of the tree shapes were replaced by angrier, threatening angles. Background painting by Thomas Woodington.

During Tarzan's battle with Sabor, shapes mirror the scene's tension and color darkens the mood. Background painting by Jean–Paul Hernandez, Joaquim Royomorales, and Patricia Millereau.

PITCHING TENTS

Having laid the groundwork, the tasks of framing the story and refining the characters began. Since the emphasis of the story would be on Tarzan's relationship with his gorilla family, it was important that the relationship be established in a logical, believable way.

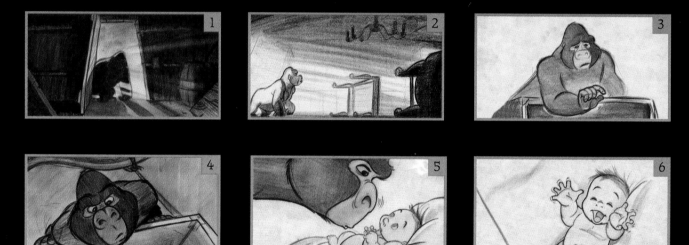

Head of story Brian Pimental created no final storyboard drawings for the film's second sequence. In this selection we see Kala, who has recently lost her own baby, enter the tree house and discover the orphaned human baby. At first merely curious about this strange little creature, Kala warms to the child when he offers her the unconditional trust and affection of the very young. In the next sequence, the attack of the leopard Sabor places Kala in the role of the baby's fierce protector, which permanently cements her bond of motherhood with the child.

"This sequence captured what I was imagining and hoped for," said Brian Pimental, praising the layout artists and animators who took what he established in the storyboard process and refined and elaborated the

In her unquestioning devotion to Tarzan and her willingness to make personal sacrifices for what is best for him, Kala embodies the movie's main theme: Family is made up more by those who love and support you rather than blood ties.

It is an understanding Kala tries to bring to young Tarzan when he asks why he is so different from the other apes.

As an adult, Tarzan once again is faced with the question of belonging when he first meets humans and discovers creatures who look like himself.

And it is an answer Tarzan discovers for himself when he is faced with the betrayal of the hunter, Clayton.

"You came back," Kerchak says when Tarzan returns to free his family.

Storyboard drawing by Jeff Snow.

"I came home," is Tarzan's quiet but decisive reply.

Storyboard drawing by Frank Nissen.

27

GETTING TO KNOW YOUR FELLOW TRAVELERS

Animators travel on this journey most closely with the character they have been assigned as their companion. Often spending many years with a single character, they sometimes begin their relationship a bit tentatively. But as they learn about their character and discover what that personality can and cannot do, they find ways to bring out his uniqueness, enriching themselves in the process.

Helping in the task of defining character, and often serving as additional inspiration, are the actors who bring their vocal talents in support of making each character a lively, distinct personality.

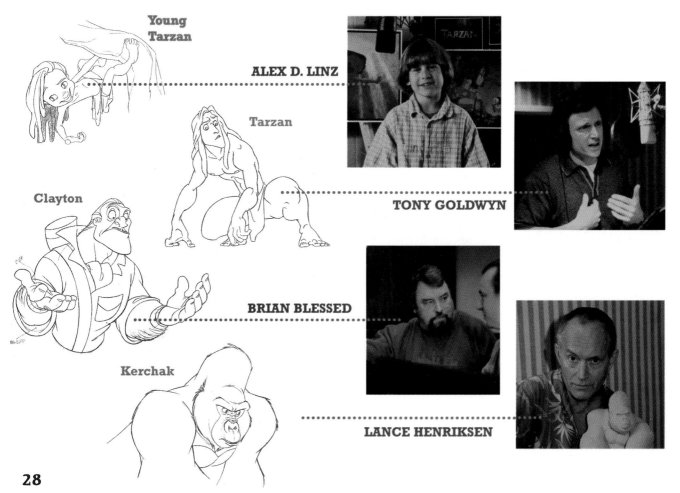

Young Tarzan

ALEX D. LINZ

Tarzan

TONY GOLDWYN

Clayton

BRIAN BLESSED

Kerchak

LANCE HENRIKSEN

Many well-known actors who come to the Disney Studio to provide the voices for the animated films remember the important part the Disney animated classics played in their own childhoods and they want to be a part of that heritage for their own children and grandchildren.

Tony Goldwyn, who speaks for the adult Tarzan, saw a voice actor's impact through an experience with his young daughter, Anna. Tony was working on a film with Nathan Lane, the voice of Timon in *The Lion King*. Nathan would call Anna each evening as Timon, greeting her with "Hakuna Matata," and according to Tony, "she was absolutely intoxicated."

GLENN CLOSE

Kala

WAYNE KNIGHT

Tantor

NIGEL HAWTHORNE

ROSIE O'DONNELL

Professor Porter

Terk

MINNIE DRIVER

Jane

Young Tarzan

"I'll be the best ape ever!"

John Ripa, supervising animator for Tarzan at his two earliest stages in life, began his studies for five-year-old Tarzan by drawing him in poses modeled by chimpanzees, getting the look of a child brought up in a family of apes.

Kala

"You'll always be in my heart."

Embodying the soul and heart of the movie, Kala experiences all the joys, frustrations, and rewards of adoptive motherhood. Glenn Close gladly accepted the role as Kala's voice. "There are very few strong mother

figures in any of the classic cartoons, so I was thrilled to be the mother ape." And, she adds, "What's lovely about Kala is that she teaches Tarzan that your worth is what's inside."

It was a creative challenge for supervising animator Russ Edmonds to portray Kala as both an ape and a character who has to act with recognizable human emotions. "What we didn't want was a person in a gorilla suit," Russ explains. "We wanted her

to look and move like a real gorilla, and gorillas move slowly. I was working on the first sequences, just trying to make her act like an ape, and realized that she could be an ape everywhere but in her face and eyes. I realized that that's where she's human—in her eyes."

Terk

"The fun has arrived."

It was natural that Tarzan's best friend among the apes was initially thought of as being a male. But as producer Bonnie Arnold explains, "When various male actors came in to test for the part, none of the voices clicked." Since the outspoken, confident personality they were looking for was so much like Rosie O'Donnell, it was suggested that she try out

for the part. It worked, and as Bonnie adds, "You don't have to be a guy to be a best friend."

Rosie even did triple-duty, providing the voice for Terk at all three ages in the film. For Terk's youngest role, Rosie had a convenient inspiration: she imitated her five-year-old niece. Reversing the physical growth process, baby Terk's design came after her adult version. Character studies by Rick Maki.

Having two adopted children herself, Rosie found the story's theme of family very appealing. "I think it's who you are nurtured and loved by, and who you nurture and love, that can define your family," Rosie states. "It has do with the heart connection."

The challenge for H. B. Lewis and supervising animator Mike Surrey was to design Terk in such a way that would distinguish her from the other apes. Part of the solution was inspired by Rosie O'Donnell. "H. B. came up with a nice face that showed that pouty little mouth Rosie has, and there was also something about the relationship of the eyes to the

mouth that helped define the character." Mike adds, "All the other gorillas have short, croppy hair. I'd taken a publicity shot of Rosie and her hair was pretty thick. I thought it was a good chance to use that as part of Terk's design, so I gave her this big tuft of hair."

Two firsts for Terk: she sees her first human other than Tarzan and she finds herself speechless.

Terk struggles to resist Tarzan's request for a favor. Rough animation by Mike Surrey.

Tantor

"Are you sure this water's sanitary? It looks questionable to me."

From that first line of dialogue, voiced by Taylor Dempsey when he was four years old, we learn that Tantor is a worrier. It's a favorite moment for supervising animator Sergio Pablos "because that's when we establish the character, and you get that right off the bat. You know exactly what this character's about."

Rough animation (above) and character study of the easily panicked pachyderm by Sergio Pablos.

The adult Tantor is steadfast to his quaking roots.

Kerchak

"Protect your family and stay away from them."

The powerful silverback Kerchak matches the strength of his body with the steadfastness of his devotion to the welfare of the ape family in his care. Lance Henriksen, who provides Kerchak's voice, immediately recognized that strength. "It's hard to imagine the power of a character like that or of an animal like that. You stand in awe of it. To try to find that energy is a challenge."

Lance found the new experience of voice work to be "a beautiful process, because of the way it grows in the collaboration between the director, the story, and the actor."

Kerchak beats on his chest to assert his authority. Rough animation by Bruce Smith.

Supervising animator Bruce Smith felt that the hardest part to animating Kerchak "was probably the restraint, since the ape leader doesn't move around a lot. It's an actor's face that you have to put on with Kerchak, keeping the character alive and actually feeling what the character is going through without showing the total expression."

Jane

"And Daddy, they took my boot!"

Jane's pell-mell recounting of her breathtaking chase from the irate baboons culminates in her indignant declaration that they absconded with her footwear. The entertaining recap of action the audience has already witnessed is an example of what a voice actor can bring to the animation process. Basically ad-libbed by Minnie Driver, the actual recording of Jane's excitable recitation was three times the length of what was used in the film. At its pared-down length, it is still one of the longest continuous sequences of character animation on record.

Referring to the recording for the baboon chase sequence, Minnie relates, "I lost my voice a couple of times. My voice would get so tired by the end of the sessions. I had to do some pretty amazing screaming." Still, she found the entire experience providing the voice for Jane as "hilarious. Just been one of my all-time favorite jobs."

Rough animation by Ken Duncan.

One of the pleasures for the audience is seeing how Jane grows through the course of the picture. Starting out properly and primly dressed as a young Victorian woman, she is nevertheless impracticably suited for a trek through the African jungle. Her independent and plucky nature breaks through, however, and as she helps Tarzan grow in his understanding of the human world outside the jungle, she also learns about his world and finds herself very much at home amid its exotic wonders.

Making Jane multidimensional and believable is what has made supervising animator Ken Duncan most proud—"that people are entertained by her, that she comes out as a multifaceted character," Ken says.

Storyboard by Glen Keane.

Professor Porter

"But you love him."

Rough animation by Dave Burgess. Clean-up by Tony Anselmo.

Filled with childlike wonder at all around him, and affectionately brought to life through the drawing skills of supervising animator Dave Burgess and the mildly befuddled vocalizations of Nigel Hawthorne,

Porter is a wise and understanding father when it comes to the welfare of his daughter, Jane.

"One of the things I wanted to do," says Dave, "was never to show Porter's open mouth. I was trying to do all the lip-synch using just the mustache, so it was quite a challenge. I used a few cheats and tried to push the shapes like crazy—but had a lot of fun with it."

Dave Burgess frequently kept Porter's hands near his face to capture his fluttery, childlike pleasure.

A sequence actually went into animation of Porter trying to locate apes disguised as one. Eventually, the filmmakers' reaction to the concept mirrored that of the apes in this early visual development art by Rowland Wilson. Porter's gorilla disguise became lost in the wilds of the editing room.

"GOOD DAY, MY DEAR."

Clayton

Tarzan initially thinks Clayton is a friend, but both Tarzan and the audience learn the full scope of the hunter's deceit when he takes the Porters and Tarzan prisoner aboard ship.

According to supervising animator Randy Haycock, the directors didn't want Clayton to be an obvious villain right from the start. They wanted a subtlety to his acting, but for a while it was difficult to get a handle on the character and how he should play. Randy relates, "There was a point when we were struggling to make Clayton charming but still a believable villain. It all came back to Brian Blessed, Clayton's voice. He had a certain quality and charisma, and when we got some of those personality traits into the character, it started to come together."

"I was born for Africa and Africa was created for me."

A hearty, though insincere, camaraderie is captured in this rough drawing by supervising animator Randy Haycock.

DEVELOPING NEW EQUIPMENT

Everyone connected with Disney's *Tarzan* wanted to enable the audience to enter and experience Tarzan's world in a totally unique way for animated filmmaking. Since the late 1930s, when Walt Disney first introduced the multiplane camera developed for *Snow White and the Seven Dwarfs*, animated features have been able to create a feeling of depth. Still, there was a degree of flatness to the images the camera was moving through. In recent years, computer animation has been able to add a more dimensional look to certain scenes, but these backgrounds often contrasted with the flatter style of the other animation elements.

When the camera moves through the *Bambi* forest, the audience never sees more than the same front surface of the trees. As amazing as that effect was in 1942, the *Tarzan* team wanted the audience to see the other sides of the trees. They also envisioned a dimensional look for *Tarzan* that would be like entering the style of painting created for the film. And they wanted to make Tarzan appear as if he was a part of his environment, not just acting in front of a two-dimensional backdrop. The process developed to achieve these three-dimensional results is called Deep Canvas.

The Deep Canvas images in *Tarzan* look as if they were created in the traditional way, but the artists in the background department were asked to put aside their paint bottles, place down their brushes, and take up the tools of the computer instead. What resulted are certain backgrounds that are undetectable from the hand-painted ones in the film, but that come breathtakingly alive as the camera twists and soars through the scene.

In addition to providing visual excitement, Deep Canvas is used to heighten a scene's emotions and support its themes. It is effectively used in the scene where Kala prepares the nest for herself and her newly adopted son. The entire background enfolds the two characters, enveloping them and embracing them, just as Kala is protecting and caring for Tarzan. Through the effect provided by Deep Canvas, we sense that the jungle will be a good, nurturing place for this youngster.

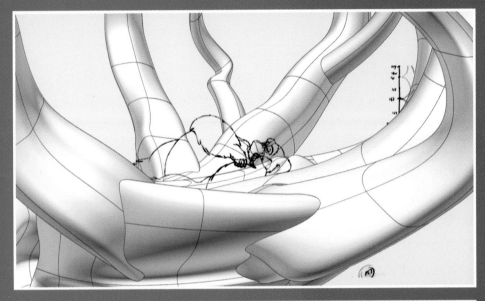

A Deep Canvas scene is created by building the basic dimensional shapes the camera will appear to move through and around (in this case the tree limbs) and positioning a line drawing of the character animation in the setting. Additional basic shapes (the vines and moss) are added. All these elements are painted to match the other backgrounds. The scene can then be filmed from various angles and positions.

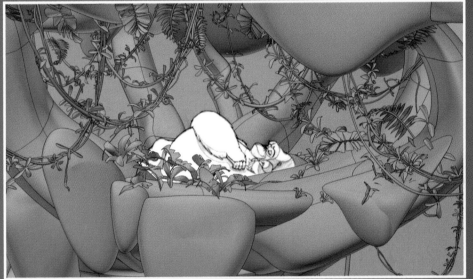

JUNGLE SOUNDS

Asong score has always helped the Disney films define character, advance the plot, and express the film's themes. Phil Collins enthusiastically shouldered the task of creating the songs for *Tarzan*.

The contributions of a film's songwriter cannot be underestimated. "Right from our earliest presentation to Phil, which was basically just an outline," Bonnie Arnold explains, "he connected with the movie's theme and understood what we were searching for. More than our film inspiring him, he inspired the movie, giving it heart and emotion through his music."

Storyboard drawing by Brian Pimental.

The film opens with the song **"Two Worlds,"** which illustrates the universal bond of family and caring shared by the shipwrecked humans and the apes living in this unfamiliar, tropical world.

Storyboard drawing by Paul Felix.

"You'll Be in My Heart" is Kala's assertion of her unwavering devotion to the strange baby she has adopted.

42

"Son of Man" follows Tarzan in his quest to be the best ape ever. It shows him developing skills by observing and mimicking jungle creatures, becoming more at home in his world, helping his family through his cleverness and abilities, and eventually reaching adulthood.

In **"Strangers Like Me"** Tarzan enthusiastically learns all he can about the human visitors and the world they come from. It also traces the growing affection Tarzan and Jane are feeling for each other.

Storyboard drawings by Glen Keane.

Storyboard by Frank Nissen.

Rosie O'Donnell had stated that she always wanted to sing in a Disney movie—and she definitely wanted to sing one of Phil's songs. She got her opportunity in the raucous number **"Trashin' the Camp,"** in which Terk and her cronies hold a jam session at the humans' camp. The music they make from the camp's paraphernalia—shaken drawers of silverware, plinked crockery, a twanged clothesline, and other makeshift "instruments"—was all performed by Collins, in a comically musical tour de force.

On-screen the sequence appears carefree and spontaneous. It was anything but that way for the filmmakers. The story team knew they wanted a rhythm piece, but they were immediately faced with the difficulty of visualizing their idea.

Storyboard by Frank Nissen.

Storyboard by Mark Walton.

Phil Collins started the process by creating a demo recording that was then drawn up on the storyboards. The visuals inspired a new demo recording, which in turn led the way to a new set of storyboards. This continued back and forth, eventually filling a dozen boards with imaginative possibilities. "Eventually everyone in the story department contributed ideas," relates Brian Pimental. Finally, Brian and the directors, Kevin and Chris, created the final storyboard by selecting the best from every version, which then was matched with Phil's final recorded version.

Storyboard by Mark Walton.

SATELLITE CAMP

WALT DISNEY FEATURE ANIMATION, PARIS, FRANCE

Tarzan AS AN ADULT

"I want to know."

Tarzan's curiosity about the world and his place in it is a quality shared by the artists at Walt Disney Feature Animation's studio in Paris, where the film's key character was animated. There's a continuous curiosity and searching by dedicated animators to find the best, most exciting ways to bring the character in their care to life.

Supervising animator Glen Keane and his team reasoned that anyone brought up from infancy by a family of animals would naturally pattern his behavior and actions after the creatures with whom he was in daily contact. They decided to make Tarzan move like an ape in a way that was more than humanly possible.

Rough animation by Kristoff Vergne. Clean–up by Philippe Briones.

In fact, this decision eliminated a traditional aspect of the animation development process: photographing live actors so that the artists can study their movements, observe how different camera angles affect body perspective, and learn how clothing drapes when a character is in action. There was no way a live actor could put himself into the twisting contortions and the extreme actions the artists planned for their animated Tarzan. The only live-action reference used for early development and study was of animal movement.

The decision not to use live-action reference became a release for the Tarzan team, enabling them to be as innovative in their animation as their imaginations would carry them. In Disney's *Tarzan*, for the first time we see a human character who walks on his knuckles like an ape. His feet are so dexterously developed that he can grasp vines with them as confidently as if they were his hands. He surfs along tree limbs, soars from dizzying heights, and roams the expanses of the jungle as naturally as the animals who have served as his role models.

Rough animation by Glen Keane.

Describing the design for Tarzan's face, Glen Keane explains, "The one word to describe Tarzan is *driven*, so his eyes had to be kind of sitting in these deep brows, tense. His nose is refined. We didn't want him to have a big chin like a superhero, so the jaw is rather narrow with a point on the chin. But at the same time I wanted it to be strong, so I gave him a lot of muscles at the back of his jaw, as if he'd been chewing bamboo all his life. Hopefully, he's handsome, in a kind of animal way."

Ultimately, the Tarzan envisioned by Disney is an individual who has developed his abilities in a unique way because of his upbringing and his talents of observation, analysis, and mimicry.

JOURNEY COMPLETED

The filmmakers reach the end of their journey when all the animation is completed, the settings have been fully rendered, visual effects that enhance the scenes and strengthen the moods are added, and final recordings of dialogue, music, and sound effects are combined with the moving images. As prints are struck of the film, the movie itself will start its own journey when its story unfolds in darkened movie houses, gathering a new set of companions who will travel with Tarzan and his friends on a great adventure.

However, as with previous Disney animated classics, such as *Pinocchio, Peter Pan, Beauty and the Beast,* and *The Lion King,* each new generation continues to discover the magic and wonder of timeless tales told through the skills, imagination, and dedicated efforts of the men and women who have embarked on the exciting adventure of animated filmmaking. This final journey is one that has no end.

The jungle echoes with Tarzan's yell after he has defeated the enemies of his family and his own doubts about where he belongs. In part a cry of victory, it is also an expression of joy for what the future holds, as he takes his place as the new leader of the apes, surrounded by those he cares for and who in turn trust and love him.

Rough animation by Glen Keane.

On a small island near the African shore, Kala discovered a strange house, high up in a tree's branches. The faint crying coming from the house had drawn Kala away from her gorilla family.

Amid the broken furniture, Kala found a baby. As she peered into his cradle, the baby giggled and reached for her. She took him in her arms and cradled him. The baby sighed and nuzzled her furry chest.

At that instant, Sabor leapt at Kala from a wooden beam above! Kala fought desperately, determined to keep the baby away from the cat's slashing claws.

As Kala fled, Sabor's paw became tangled in a rope. Kala clutched the baby closer and raced toward the safety of her family.

The apes gathered around Kala and gaped at the strange, furless baby.

Kerchak, leader of the ape family, loomed over them. "I cannot let you put our family in danger," he declared.

"Does he look dangerous to you?" asked Kala, holding up the cooing infant.

Kerchak hesitated. "Was it alone?" he asked.

"Yes," said Kala. "Sabor killed his family."

"Well, then you may keep him," he said, reluctantly.

"I know he'll be a good son," said Kala.

"I said he could stay," replied Kerchak. "That doesn't make him my son."

Kala named the baby Tarzan.

Over the next few years, Tarzan grew up strong and curious, swinging from vines and mimicking the ways of the jungle animals.

One day Terk and her other gorilla buddies were playing near the lagoon. Tarzan begged to join them. "I'd love to hang out with you," Terk whispered to Tarzan. "But the guys, they need a little convincing."

"What do I gotta do?" asked Tarzan.

"Well . . . you gotta . . . uh . . . go get an elephant hair," Terk said.

Tarzan dove into the water! He'd show those guys he wasn't too little to play with them. He latched onto an elephant's tail and plucked a hair.

The elephants were so frightened they began to stampede—right through the gorillas' feeding grounds!

When things finally settled down, Kerchak was angry. "What happened?" he demanded.

"It was my fault," said Tarzan.

"I should have known," said Kerchak. "Stampeding the elephants. He almost killed someone."

"He's only a child," argued Kala. "He'll learn."

"You can't learn to be one of us!" shouted Kerchak.

Upset, Tarzan stared at his reflection in a jungle pool.

When Kala caught up with him, Tarzan held his hands against hers. "Why am I so different?" he asked.

"Close your eyes," whispered Kala. "Now forget what you see." She put Tarzan's hand to his chest. "What do you feel?"

"My heart?" asked Tarzan.

"Come here," she said. She pressed his ear to her chest.

"Your heart," said Tarzan.

"See," said Kala. "Inside we're the same. Kerchak just can't see that."

"I'll make him see it," said Tarzan, beating his chest. "I'll be the best ape ever!"

"Oh, I bet you will," said Kala, with a smile.

As the years went by, Tarzan, Terk, and Tantor, the elephant, grew to be great friends. One day, while Terk and Tantor were wrestling, Tarzan sensed something in the bushes. Just as he turned, Sabor leaped at him!

Kerchak appeared and grabbed the snarling leopard and threw her to the ground. Angry, Sabor raked Kerchak with her claws and moved in for the kill.

Tarzan swung between Sabor and Kerchak. The gorillas gasped as they saw Sabor knock Tarzan into a deep pit. When they reappeared, Tarzan was victorious!

But the celebration was short-lived because the gorillas heard gunshots and they raced deeper into the jungle.

Tarzan swung through the trees toward the strange sounds. He saw humans for the first time.

"Clayton, wha-what is it?" asked Professor Porter.

"I thought I saw something," replied the hunter.

"Mr. Clayton," said Jane, "my father and I came on this expedition to study gorillas, and your shooting might be scaring them off."

Then, Jane saw a baby baboon.

"Wait! Hold still!" She whipped out her pencil and sketchbook. The baboon snatched the book and ran.

When Jane caught up, the little baboon was admiring the portrait she had drawn. She pulled it from his hands, and he began to cry. The grown-up baboons moved in!

From a treetop, Tarzan watched as Jane ran, followed by hundreds of baboons. As Jane tried to jump across a deep chasm, Tarzan swung down from his tree and scooped her up.

"Oh . . . I'm flying!" Jane cried.

Tarzan set her safely on a branch and began to study the curious new creature.

"Don't come any closer," Jane pleaded. Tarzan reached out to touch her cheek.

"How dare you!" gasped Jane. She tried to slap him, but he caught her hand. Gently, he peeled off her glove and held his palm up to hers.

Tarzan leaned forward and put his ear to her chest. "Oh, oh, um," she stammered.

Hearing a distant gunshot, Jane asked, "Can you take me to my camp?"

Tarzan took Jane by the waist, and off they swung. When they arrived, they found the camp in shambles.

"Gorillas!" cried Jane, thrilled to catch a glimpse of the creatures she had come so far to study. To her amazement, she saw that Tarzan knew them!

As Clayton and her father approached, the gorillas disappeared into the jungle. Tarzan cast one more glance at Jane and then he fled, too.

Far away from the humans' camp, Kerchak told his family, "We will avoid the strangers."

"Why are you threatened by anyone different from you?" argued Tarzan.

"Protect this family and stay away from them," demanded Kerchak.

Upset and confused, Tarzan climbed a high tree and spent the night alone.

The next day, as Jane was describing the strange ape-man to her father and Clayton, Tarzan himself dropped down from the trees.

"Jane," said Tarzan.

"Yes, hello," answered Jane.

"Fascinating!" cried Porter. "He could be the missing link!"

"Or our link to the gorillas!" said Clayton, slyly.

For many days, Jane taught Tarzan about the human world. And Tarzan showed her the wonders of the jungle.

"Tarzan," said Jane, "will you take us to the gorillas?"

"I can't," replied Tarzan.

The next morning, Tarzan saw men packing up Jane and Porter's belongings and carrying them off to a ship.

"Tarzan!" cried Jane. "I was so afraid you wouldn't come in time. Daddy

and I hope that you'll come with us."

"Go see England today, come home tomorrow?" asked Tarzan.

"Oh, no. It would be very difficult to come back . . . ever," whispered Jane.

"Jane must stay with Tarzan," said Tarzan.

"Here? No, I can't—" Jane rushed away, crying.

Clayton put his arm around Tarzan. "If only she could have spent more time with the gorillas."

"If Jane sees gorillas, she stays?" asked Tarzan.

Tarzan asked Terk and Tantor to lure Kerchak away from the other gorillas. Then Tarzan led the humans to the nesting area.

"Isn't she beautiful?" whispered Jane, seeing Kala under a shelter of bushes.

"She's my mother," said Tarzan.

"Th-this is your mother?" asked Jane. Kala and the others shrank deeper into the bushes. Tarzan knelt down, saying soothing ape words. Jane and Porter imitated him. Soon the gorillas came out of their hiding places.

Jane and Porter were delighted, but Clayton only checked his map and drew an "X" to mark the gorillas' location.

Suddenly, Terk and Tantor came crashing through the bushes with Kerchak right behind them.

When Kerchak saw the humans with his family, he was furious.

Clayton lifted his rifle to fire. Kerchak charged him and knocked his gun away.

Tarzan wrestled Kerchak off Clayton and struggled to hold the mighty ape. "Go!" he shouted at the humans.

Kerchak roared in anger as the humans fled.

"Kerchak, I'm sorry," said Tarzan.

"I asked you to protect our family!" cried Kerchak. "And you betrayed us all."

Tarzan retreated into the jungle. He sat alone, looking at the ship in the distance.

Kala found him.

"I'm so confused," Tarzan said sadly.

"Come," said Kala. "There's something I should have showed you long ago."

She led Tarzan to the tree house. Tarzan stared at the cradle. On the floor he found a portrait of two humans and a baby.

"Is this me?" he asked. "And this is my father . . . and my . . . "

"Now you know," said Kala, fighting back tears. "I just want you to be happy . . . whatever you decide."

Minutes later, Tarzan stepped out of the tree house, dressed in his father's clothes. Kala gasped. "No matter where I go, you will always be my mother," said Tarzan, embracing her.

Tarzan cast one last look behind at the beautiful jungle that had been his home. Then he climbed aboard the ship, bound for England.

Sailors quickly seized Tarzan. "Clayton!" cried Tarzan.

"So sorry about the rude welcome," said Clayton, "but I couldn't have you making a scene when we put your furry friends in their cages."

"Why?" asked Tarzan.

"For three hundred pounds sterling a head!" exclaimed Clayton. "And I couldn't have done it without you."

Tarzan let out a cry of despair. Clayton ordered the sailors to lock Tarzan in the hold with Jane and Porter.

On shore, Terk and Tantor heard Tarzan's cry. Tantor charged toward the ship with Terk in tow.

Inside the hold, Tarzan pounded on the hull.

"Clayton betrayed us all," said Jane. "I am so sorry."

"No, I did this. I betrayed my family," cried Tarzan.

Suddenly the ship keeled over, throwing them all to one side.

"What was that?" asked Jane.

A huge elephant foot crashed through the deck.

"Tantor!" shouted Tarzan. He scrambled through the hole his friend had made and helped Jane and Porter up to the deck.

Tarzan raced through the jungle to rescue the gorillas. The others followed close behind.

At the gorilla nesting grounds, Clayton and his men were rounding up the apes and throwing them into cages.

Clayton pointed his gun at Kerchak. "I think this one will be better off stuffed." Then Clayton noticed Tarzan and turned to fire at him, but Kerchak leaped between Tarzan and the bullet. Wounded, the large ape fell.

Clayton chased after Tarzan, following him up into the trees. They struggled and Clayton fell to his death.

Tarzan raced back to Kerchak. "Forgive me," Tarzan said.

"No, Tarzan, I misjudged you," said Kerchak. "Our family will look to you now. Take care of them, my son."

Everyone bowed, mourning the death of their leader. Then Tarzan rose and beat his chest, signaling his role as the apes' new leader.

Early the next morning, Tarzan made his way to the beach to say farewell to Jane and Porter. "I will miss you, Jane," Tarzan said softly.

As they were being rowed to the ship, Porter said, "Jane, dear, I can't help feeling that you should stay."

"But I belong in England, with you," protested Jane.

"But you love him," said Porter. "Go on."

Jane jumped out of the boat and splashed through the water.

Porter smiled. "Captain," he said, "tell them you never found us. After all, people get lost in the jungle every day." He followed his daughter to shore.

Tarzan kissed Jane, while all the apes looked on.

Kala reached out her hand to welcome Jane, as Tarzan led his family back into the jungle.

THE LIFE OF EDGAR RICE BURROUGHS

Edgar Rice Burroughs, like Walt Disney with Mickey Mouse, created a legendary character that is known in almost every corner of the world—Tarzan of the Apes. Burroughs was born September 1, 1875, in Chicago, Illinois. Burroughs witnessed the turn of the century in the prime of his youth, living his life in the spirit of a young explorer of his era. His actions, deeds, and thoughts emphasized his love of adventure and his passion for creativity.

At different times in his life, Ed Burroughs trekked the American west as a private in the 7th U.S. Cavalry, rode horses and herded cattle on his brothers' ranch, dredged for gold on a river boat—also with his brothers, carried mail on horseback, was an alderman, and even served some time as a railroad policeman.

Above: **A childhood photograph of ERB (approximately 7-10 years old).**

Left: **Though he was often overly modest about his own talents, Edgar Rice Burroughs always tried to assure that his most famous fictional character, Tarzan, was portrayed accurately. This photograph was taken in 1934.**

Young Ed Burroughs (first row, first on the left) in his high school football team photo at Michigan Military Academy.

But even with a resume that might look exciting to many a child, Ed had a hard time finding his professional niche in life. In his teens, Ed seemed to have a penchant for getting into trouble on a regular basis at the small Michigan Military Academy he attended. He found some solace there in playing football and developing his skills as a horseman. He developed remarkable skill as a trick rider: bareback, Cossack, and Greco-Roman.

Many years after his short-lived career as a police officer had ended, Edgar Rice Burroughs pulled his old uniform out of the closet and even sported a fake mustache as he hammed it up for this photograph.

Edgar Rice Burroughs, war correspondent and grandfather, shares a happy moment with his grandsons in 1944. From left to right: John Ralston Burroughs (son of Jack Burroughs); ERB; James Michael Pierce (son of Joan Burroughs Pierce); Danton Burroughs (son of Jack Burroughs).

In 1900, Ed married his childhood sweetheart and neighbor, Emma Hulbert. Eight years later, Emma gave birth to their first child, Joan. His first son, Hulbert, was born in 1909 and his second son, John Coleman ("Jack"), was born in 1913.

Whether due to his own impatience, his lack of discipline, or simply a desire to control his own destiny, Ed found it difficult to stay with any of the numerous jobs he worked at before turning to writing. Because of his constant search for autonomy, financial stability eluded him.

Ironically, Ed did not venture into a career as a writer until he was well into his thirties. At that point, the young father, struggling desperately to make ends meet and to support his growing family, wrote the first half of a story in the hopes of gaining some added income. He was surprised at the enthusiasm of the magazine's editor, who asked that he finish the story and send it to him. The story entitled "Under the Moon of Mars" was published in six parts in the *All-Story* magazine beginning in February 1912. Ed was thirty-six years old.

That same year the *All-Story* magazine paid Ed seven hundred dollars to publish a story entitled "Tarzan of the Apes." By 1914, A. C. McClurg & Company, after previously rejecting it, published "Tarzan of the Apes" in book form because of reader demand after it had been published serially in numerous newspapers from coast-to-coast. The ape-man was on his way toward becoming the legend he is today.

"Tarzan of the Apes" was first published in the *All-Story* magazine, October 1912 (copyright 1912, Munsey Publications).

Edgar Rice Burroughs used the pen name of Normal Bean when he first started writing stories.

What exactly made Tarzan so appealing? Ed modestly confessed his dismay at his hero's popularity. Yet it was also clear that Ed loved and admired the character he had created in Tarzan. He always maintained that Tarzan was a highly intelligent human being. It was chance that led Tarzan to be raised in an African jungle by a family of fictitious apes, but it was his own skill and quick wit that helped him excel in that environment.

This picture of Tarzan and the Golden Lion was created by Roy G. Krenkel. It is still used on the letterhead for Edgar Rice Burroughs, Inc.

Jack Burroughs (ERB's son) poses with his father in front of a painting Jack created for the cover of a book featuring two of ERB's stories, 1937.

Ed saw Tarzan as strong but graceful, well-muscled but lithe. The author often voiced his opinions on the subject to both the illustrators of his books and the producers and directors of Tarzan films. "It is true that in the stories I often speak of Tarzan as the 'giant ape-man,' but that is because I am rather prone to superlatives," Ed once wrote. "My conception of him is a man a little over six feet tall and built more like a panther than an elephant."

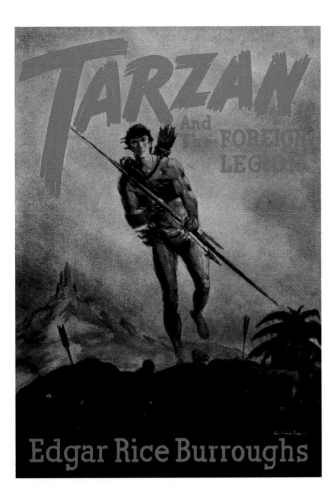

This dust jacket for Edgar Rice Burroughs's novel *Tarzan and the Foreign Legion* features the artwork of John Coleman ("Jack") Burroughs, Ed's son.

Edgar Rice Burroughs's bookplate, designed by his nephew, Studley O. Burroughs.

Tarzan Sunday and daily comic strips have been published in dozens of newspapers and in many different languages.

From the beginning, Tarzan's popularity grew tremendously. In 1918, the first Tarzan film was produced. In 1929, a Tarzan comic strip was created. In later years, there were Tarzan radio programs. Tarzan began appearing on game boards, posters, Tarzan Club memorabilia, collectible cards, buttons, bracelets, ice cream cups, pins, and numerous other licensed products.

Throughout it all, Ed struggled to maintain Tarzan's integrity. Always quick to use humor and modesty in his writings, Ed nevertheless was steadfast in his defense of Tarzan. He kept the rights to all the Tarzan stories, incorporated himself in 1923 and did his best to maintain a close watch on the items produced in support of his most popular fictional character.

A family photograph taken at Ed's Malibu home in 1934. First row (from left to right): ERB's first wife, Emma; Joanne Pierce in the lap of her mother, Joan Burroughs Pierce. Second row (left to right): ERB; Jim Pierce; Jack Burroughs; Hulbert Burroughs.

ERB with his family (from left to right): Joan, Hulbert, ERB, Emma, and Jack, about 1924.

Ed loved to involve family members in the development of Tarzan materials because he knew they would remain true to the character and his world. Ed's nephew, Studley Burroughs, and Ed's son John Coleman Burroughs were both trained artists and illustrated many of the Tarzan books, as well as other novels written by Ed. John Coleman Burroughs, or "Jack" as he was called by his family, often used family members as models when he created and designed the characters in his father's books. Today, Jack's son Danton is the director of Edgar Rice Burroughs, Inc., the corporation that manages the rights to the stories and characters created by Edgar Rice Burroughs.

John Coleman Burroughs often asked family members to pose for the artwork he created for his father's novels. In this picture, Jack's wife, Jane, poses as Dejah Thoris, the love interest in Ed's John Carter of Mars series of stories.

ERB with his longtime secretary and manager, Cyril Ralph Rothmund, in 1937.

ERB with his family in 1930. From left to right: Hulbert, Emma, ERB, Jack, and Joan.

In the mid-1930s Jack and Ed exchanged ideas regarding the creation of an animated Tarzan cartoon. This was another project over which Ed maintained close control. In 1936, he wrote to Jack, "It [the cartoon] must be good. It must approximate Disney excellence." Ironically, the letter was written over sixty years before Disney's animated version of Tarzan reached the big screen.

In 1919 Ed used his earnings as a writer to purchase the 550-acre estate of the late General Harrison Gray Otis in southern California. He renamed the ranch "Tarzana" in honor of the fictional character who had brought him at long last to a place of financial security. Later a portion of that site became the city of Tarzana, which still carries the same name.

This photo taken in the 1930s shows Edgar Rice Burroughs seated at the same desk that his grandson Danton uses to this day. Danton currently serves as director of Edgar Rice Burroughs, Inc.

In the mornings, Burroughs would ride his horse down the hill of Tarzana Ranch to his private office, where he would create and write about such characters as Tarzan, John Carter of Mars, David Innes of Pellucidar, and countless other brave and dauntless heroes and heroines. In the evenings, he often treated his family and his neighbors to the most recent Tarzan films in the screening room of the main house.

Edgar Rice Burroughs often rode his horse down the hill to his office at Tarzana Ranch.

This aerial photograph of Edgar Rice Burroughs's beloved ranch home in southern California was taken in 1922. Ed named the ranch "Tarzana" in honor of his most famous fictional character.

Photographs and personal letters from that era testify to the fact that Ed was no stranger to the glamorous world of Hollywood. The numerous films based on Tarzan brought Ed in contact with many famous actors and actresses, including the most popular Tarzan actor, Johnny Weissmuller. When Ed built a golf course on his ranch and formed the El Caballero Country Club around it, he frequently mingled there with the rich and famous.

Johnny Weissmuller poses with Edgar Rice Burroughs, September 12, 1932. Weissmuller starred as Tarzan in twelve motion pictures.

This 1932 photograph was signed by Buster Keaton, who wrote, "To Edgar Rice Burroughs—from the guy who should have played Tarzan."

Emma Burroughs (second row, first on left) poses with her husband, ERB (second row, fifth from left), and the cast of *The Adventures of Tarzan*, 1921.

ERB with Maureen O'Sullivan in 1932 at Burroughs's Tarzana Golf Course. O'Sullivan played Jane in several of the Tarzan films.

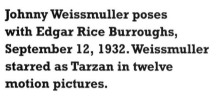

A lover of cars and travel, Edgar Rice Burroughs poses in 1934 in front of his Cord automobile.

Ed continued to seek out adventure in real life, as he wrote prolifically of imaginary worlds and newly invented characters.

He had a great love for animals and would not permit hunters on his property. He became a deputy sheriff so he could more easily enforce his no-hunting rules.

At the age of fifty-eight, Ed decided to take up flying. Later, after a sad divorce from Emma, he moved to Hawaii with his second wife, Florence Gilbert. He was living there when he and his son Hulbert witnessed the Japanese attack on Pearl Harbor that launched the United States into World War II. Shortly thereafter, he volunteered and was appointed a war correspondent by the United Press, covering the Pacific theater of operations. During this exciting time, Ed was sent to Australia, where he was invited to go along on some bombing runs by Brigadier General Truman H. Landon, commanding general of the 7th Bomber Command, Air Force.

ERB (holding binoculars) witnessing the Japanese attack on Pearl Harbor, December 7, 1941.

Edgar Rice Burroughs worked as a war correspondent during World War II.

After his death on March 19, 1950, at the age of seventy-four, his family honored his final request and buried Edgar Rice Burroughs's ashes under a big black walnut tree that shaded the offices on his beloved Tarzana Ranch. Although his life had ended, Edgar Rice Burroughs's fantastic stories and adored characters continue to live on in the hearts and minds of his fans around the world.

ERB poses in the black walnut tree in front of his Tarzana offices in the 1940s. Burroughs maintained his love of the outdoors throughout his life. (Photographs courtesy of Edgar Rice Burroughs, Inc. © 1999 Edgar Rice Burroughs, Inc. and Used by Permission)

To Joyce

Library of Congress Cataloging-in-Publication Data

Arnosky, Jim.
Beachcombing / by Jim Arnosky.—1st ed. p. cm.
Summary: Illustrations and text describe some of the many things that can be found on a walk
along a beach, including coconuts, shark teeth, jellyfish, crabs, and different kinds of shells.
ISBN 0-525-47104-9
1. Seashore biology—Juvenile literature. 2. Beachcombing—Juvenile literature.
[1. Beachcombing. 2. Seashore ecology. 3. Ecology.] I. Title.
QH95.7.A76 2004
578.769'9—dc22 2003062484

Published in the United States by Dutton Children's Books,
a division of Penguin Young Readers Group
345 Hudson Street, New York, New York 10014
www.penguin.com

Designed by Gloria Cheng

Manufactured in China
First Edition
1 3 5 7 9 10 8 6 4 2

BEACHCOMBING
exploring the seashore

by Jim Arnosky

DUTTON CHILDREN'S BOOKS ◎ NEW YORK

Beachcombing is walking slowly near the ocean, looking for bits and pieces of nature the waves wash in.

It is wading ankle-deep in the foamy surf and pretending that you're all alone on your very own tropical island.

The Complete Beachcomber

To be a beachcomber, all you need is sunblock (with an SPF of 30 or higher), a broad-brimmed hat to shade your head, sunglasses to protect your eyes, and a bucket to carry shells and other treasures you find.

SEASHELLS

Beachcombing is collecting colorful seashells and learning all their names. Remember, each and every seashell once housed a marine animal. Collect only empty shells. If you find any shells that are still inhabited, return them to the water.

Calico Clam

Cockleshell

Slipper

Mussel

Worm Shell

Whelk

Olive

Cardita

Tulip

Sea Urchin

Razor Clam

Pen

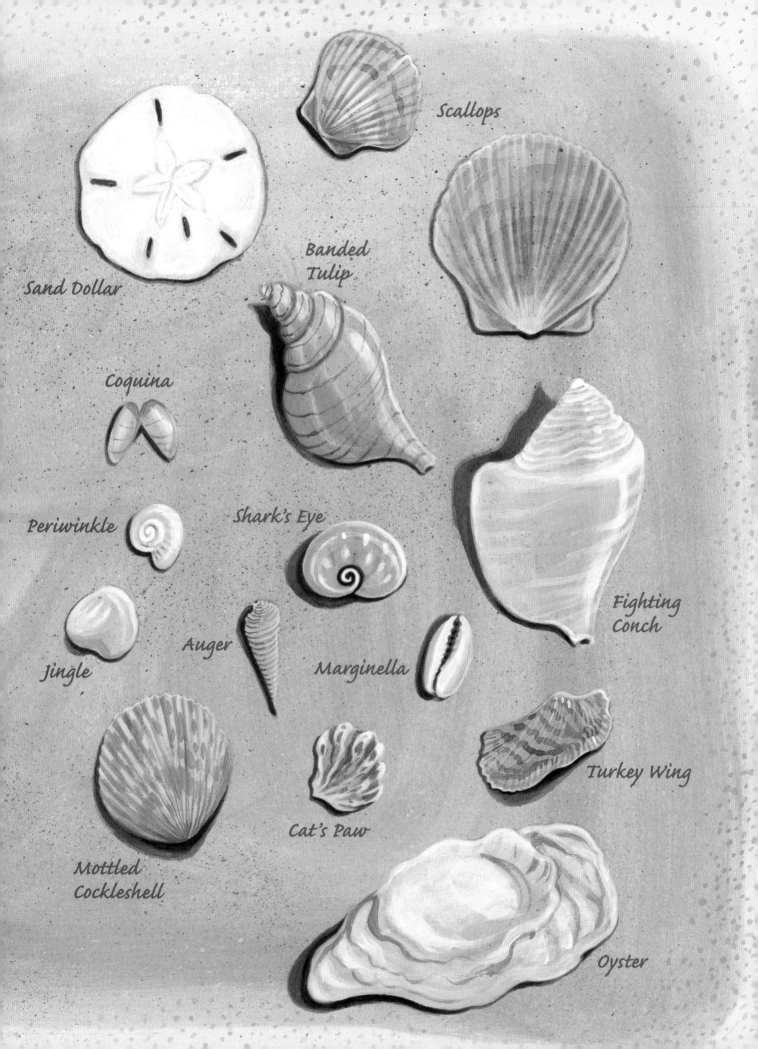

Scallops

Sand Dollar

Banded
Tulip

Coquina

Periwinkle

Shark's Eye

Fighting
Conch

Jingle

Auger

Marginella

Turkey Wing

Cat's Paw

Mottled
Cockleshell

Oyster

CRABS

Among the galaxy of seashells strewn along the shoreline, you may find broken bits and pieces of crab
shells. If you are lucky, you will find an entire crab
shell, complete with legs attached, recently
shed by a living crab.

crab claw

crab carapace

shed intact shell

Watch for live crabs in the water.
Living crabs such as this Blue Crab
will pinch you if you accidentally
step on them.

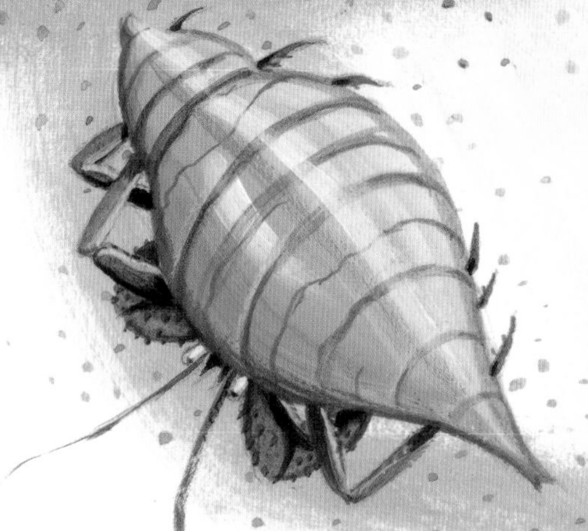

Blue Crab

Hermit Crab

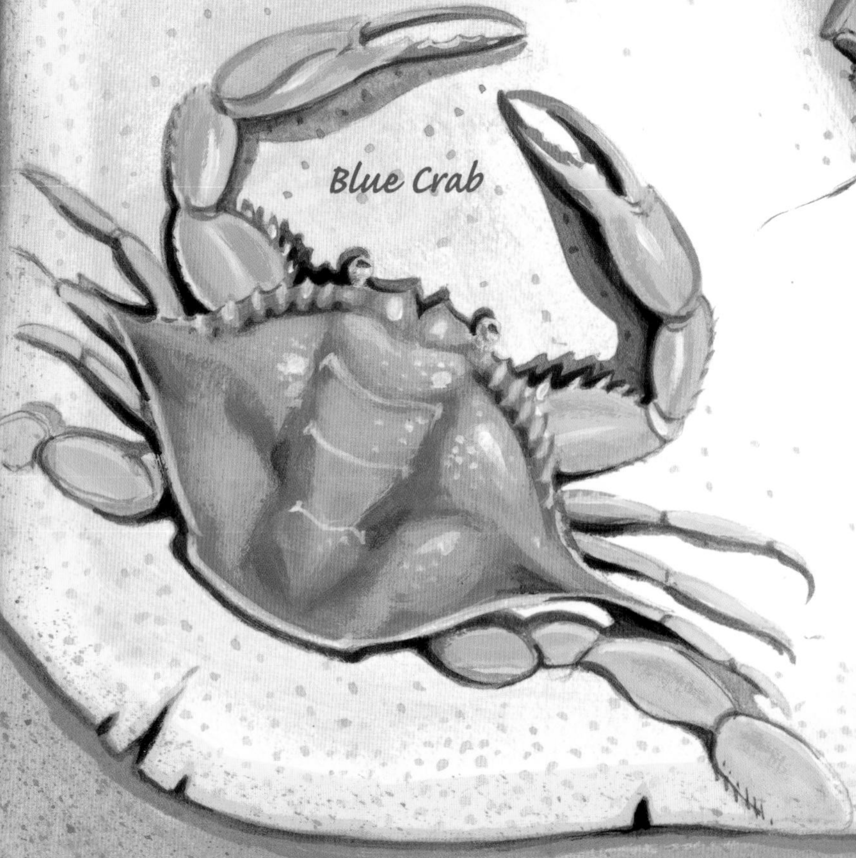

Hermit Crabs inhabit the empty
shells of other creatures. This
Hermit Crab is living inside the
abandoned shell of a Banded
Tulip Snail.

On beaches left exposed by low tide, you might see tiny crabs scurrying out of their holes, foraging for bits of food. The small pale-yellow crabs are Ghost Crabs. The darker, purplish crabs are Fiddler Crabs, named for their one large claw that resembles a violin or fiddle being held high.

When you see a Ghost Crab or Fiddler Crab, sit quietly and watch for more. Soon you will be surrounded by tiny crabs venturing out of their holes.

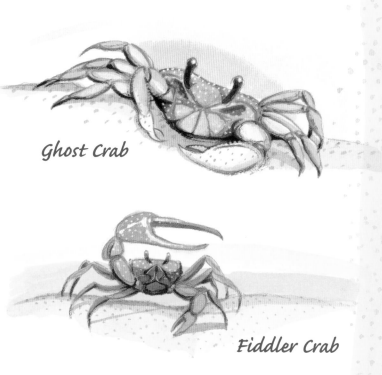

Ghost Crab

Fiddler Crab

Many species of crabs can be identified by shape alone. Here are eight crab shapes to look for in the water or on the beach.

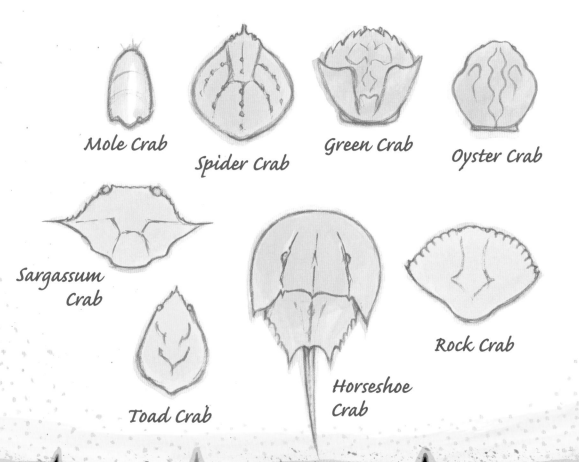

Mole Crab

Spider Crab

Green Crab

Oyster Crab

Sargassum Crab

Toad Crab

Horseshoe Crab

Rock Crab

HORSESHOE CRAB

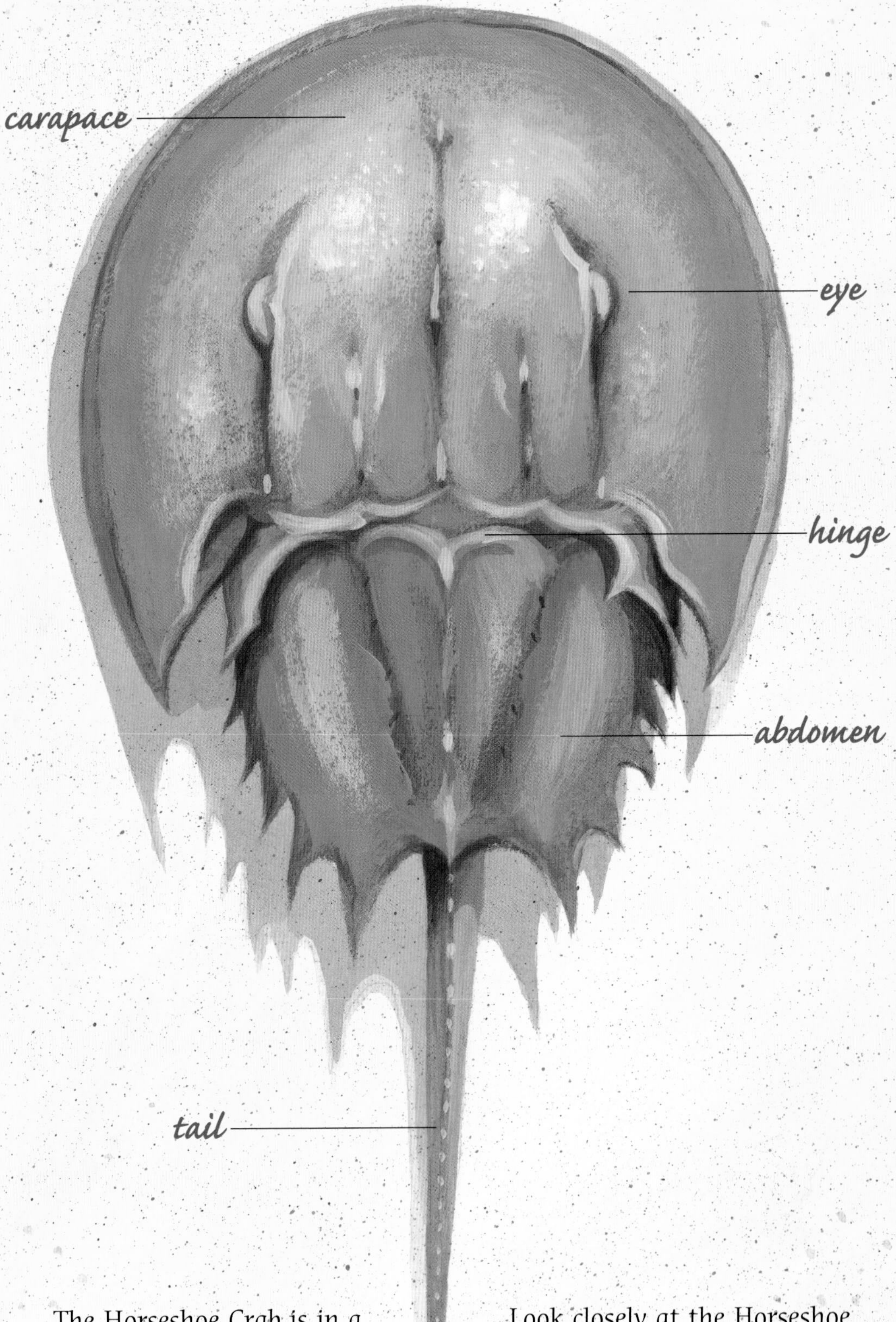

carapace ——————

eye —————————

hinge —————————

abdomen —————————

tail —————————

The Horseshoe Crab is in a class by itself. Horseshoe Crabs have existed virtually unchanged for 400 million years!

Look closely at the Horseshoe Crab's helmetlike carapace. Its compound eyes are looking back at you.

The Horseshoe Crab is the biggest crab a beachcomber is likely to find. It doesn't pinch like other crabs. It is okay to gently flip one over with your toe to see the underside. Just make sure you gently flip it back the way it was.

Like all crabs, Horseshoe Crabs shed their shells to grow. Finding a shed shell that's intact is something special. Finding the shed shell of a baby Horseshoe Crab is a treasure.

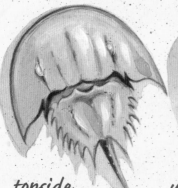

topside   *underside*

Shed Horseshoe Crab shell shown actual size

This is the smallest shed Horseshoe Crab shell I have ever found.

Can you find one smaller?

What are those ghostly, gooey-looking forms on the wet sand? They are jellyfish, washed in and stranded by the tide. I never step on stranded jellyfish. Nor will I touch them with my hands. Many species of jellyfish can sting.

I do enjoy looking at them, and I try to sketch the shape of every one I see. Here are some of the jellyfish shapes I found one morning on one beach.

Portuguese Man-of-War and seaweed

Occasionally, Portuguese Man-of-War jellyfish will wash ashore. A sting from the tentacles of this sea creature can be very painful. Man-of-War jellyfish are easy to identify. They look like little blue balloons. If you see one on the sand or tangled in seaweed, stay away! Even the tiniest Man-of-War jellyfish has long tentacles that can sting you.

In the water, a Man-of-War jellyfish floats on the surface with its long, food-catching tentacles hanging down.

A CORAL BEACH

Wherever there is a coral reef offshore, the beach will be bright white, because it is made up entirely of broken bits of sun-bleached coral.

Beachcombers on coral beaches have to wear wading shoes or sneakers to protect their feet from sharp pieces of coral.

Even the large boulders you see on a coral beach are actually chunks of fossilized coral reef. Look closely at coral beach boulders and you will see the different shapes and patterns of coral species that once lived out on the reef.

Besides seashells and crab shells, there are things unique to a coral sea that wash up on the beach. Here are some of the more unusual things beachcombers can find on a coral beach.

Small chunk of Star Coral

Branched Sponge

Colorful bits and pieces of Branch Coral

Large, vase-shaped Sponge

Branch Coral intact with broken base

WHERE DO COCONUTS COME FROM?

Question: *Where do coconuts come from?*
Answer: *Palm trees.*

Question: *Where do palm trees come from?*
Answer: *Coconuts.*

Beachcombers occasionally find coconuts washed ashore. Almost all have floated a great distance from some faraway place.

Every coconut you see onshore has fallen from a palm tree somewhere. And every palm tree growing on the beach has sprouted from a coconut that once washed ashore.

This is a newly sprouted coconut palm. If the waves don't unearth it and the wind doesn't blow it away, it will grow to be a magnificent shoreline tree.

Where do coconut pirates come from?
I have no idea!

BEACH BIRDS

A beachcomber's constant companions are the ever-present beach birds. Beach birds search the wet beach for freshly washed-in bits of food, such as tiny crabs or shellfish.

Sandpipers, small and large, run from wave wash to wave wash to catch crabs burrowing into the wet sand. Sandpipers will walk behind or ahead of you, always keeping just enough distance from you to feel safe.

Sandpipers come in sizes that range from short and small to big and tall. All species of sandpipers are mottled brown or gray in color.

Of all the birds on the beach, my favorites are the gulls, terns, and skimmers. Gulls are the boldest of birds. Wherever a gull lands, it makes the place its own. I admire that. Terns glide on the wind over the waves so gracefully, they make me wish I could do it with them. And I love watching Black Skimmers speed along, using their long bills to slice through the water surface and snap up small fish.

Herring Gull

Ring-billed Gull

Common Tern

Laughing Gull

Royal Tern

Black Skimmer

SOME SPECIAL FINDS

Walk the length of a beach one way. Then turn and walk back, looking down at the very same spots. The view from the opposite direction always reveals something you missed before.

This is when a beachcomber finds the most unexpected treasures, such as Mermaid's Purses and Sea Beans.

This is the egg case of a skate, also known as a Mermaid's Purse.

Whelk egg cases in a chain

Depending on the size of the individual whelk they came from, these chainlike egg cases can be up to ten times larger than the one pictured here.

Mermaid's Purses are actually the leathery egg cases of either stingrays, skates, or sharks. Collect only those that are empty and hard. Any that are soft and still have contents should be put back into the water.

Other curious-looking egg cases you may find are those of whelks and conchs. These egg cases resemble extra-long rattlesnake rattles. When thoroughly dried, they rattle when shaken.

Sea Beans look a lot like large, flattened chestnuts. They are the seeds of trees that grow along the banks of the Amazon River in South America. Because they're as beautiful as they are rare and have drifted such great distances, Sea Beans are highly prized by beachcombers.

Sea Beans shown actual size

Sea Beans can be flat or round.

This curious-looking thing is actually a small coconut.

Broken tooth or tusk

SHARK TEETH

Most of the shark teeth we see are the big, scary-looking ones in the mouths of sharks on TV or in plastic replicas of huge sharks on display in restaurants and museums. However, sharks come in all sizes, and so do shark teeth.

Sharks have been swimming in the oceans for millions of years. In all that time, they have changed very little. The fossilized teeth of ancient shark species are similar to the teeth of sharks alive today.

Where the beach sand is dark gray in color and peppered with lots of black grit, the beach is most likely fossiliferous. Some of the black bits in the sand could be fossilized shark teeth!

Tooth of a living Great White Shark

Tooth of a living Mako Shark

SHARK EXHIBIT

This model shows a Great White Shark ready to bite. Sometimes when a shark bites, a tooth breaks off and sinks to the bottom of the ocean. Those that wash ashore are found by beachcombers.

Scoop a handful of wet sand and search through the broken shells and sand pebbles for tiny fossilized shark teeth. Here is one morning's gleanings of shark teeth on a famously fossiliferous Gulf Coast beach.

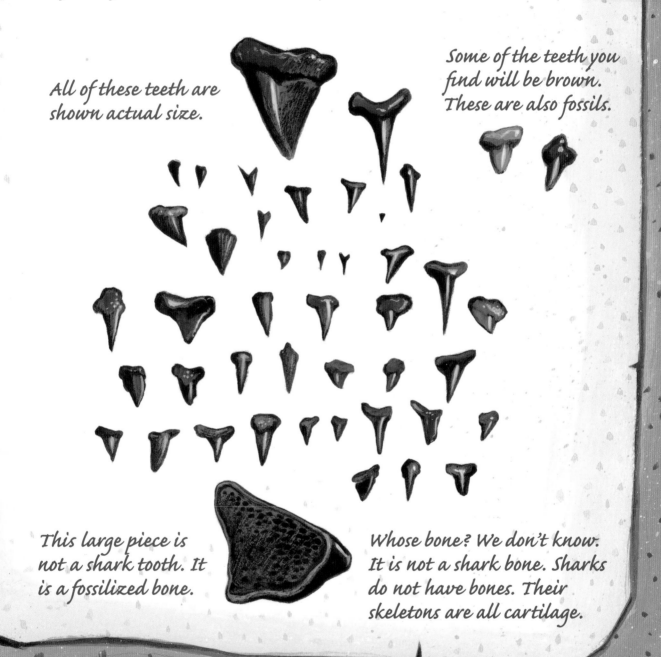

All of these teeth are shown actual size.

Some of the teeth you find will be brown. These are also fossils.

This large piece is not a shark tooth. It is a fossilized bone.

Whose bone? We don't know. It is not a shark bone. Sharks do not have bones. Their skeletons are all cartilage.

Finding a pure white tooth from a living shark, such as this large Tiger Shark tooth, is extremely rare. Most shark teeth you find will be fossilized and black or gray in color.

The beach is one place that is new every day.
The tide washes in, and it washes away.

A beachcomber can walk the same beach again and
again and always find something new and wonderful.

Author's Note

To research this book, my wife, Deanna, and I visited twenty-six different beaches along the Atlantic and Gulf coasts. We walked the shorelines looking for things that made each beach special—the color of the sand, the condition of the washed-in shells, and the variety of shorebirds. And when we had walked as far as we wanted to go in one direction, we turned and followed our own footprints back to where we had started. We sat and watched the ocean for the splashes of fish and the distant shapes of boats. We waded ankle-deep in the waves. It was wonderful!

I made lots of little sketches in my notebook. We took pictures of everything, even our own footprints in the sand. When we got back home again, I used my sketches and photographs to create the paintings in *Beachcombing*. I hope this book helps you to enjoy your visits to the seashore—real or imagined—as much as we have enjoyed ours.

Jim Arnosky

More Books for Beachcombers and Naturalists

Arnosky, Jim. *All About Sharks*. New York: Scholastic, 2003.

——. *Field Trips: Bug Hunting, Animal Tracking, Bird-watching, Shore Walking*. New York: HarperCollins, 2002.

Arthur, Alex. *Eyewitness: Shell*. New York: DK Publishing, 2000.

Berger, Melvin, and Gilda Berger. *What Makes an Ocean Wave? Questions and Answers About Oceans and Ocean Life*. New York: Scholastic Reference, 2001.

Cerullo, Mary M. *The Truth About Dangerous Sea Creatures*. San Francisco: Chronicle Books, 2003.

Davies, Nicola. *Surprising Sharks*. Boston: Candlewick, 2003.

George, Twig. *Jellies*. Brookfield, CT: Millbrook Press, 2001.

Greenaway, Theresa. *The Secret World of Crabs*. Austin, TX: Raintree/Steck-Vaughn, 2001.

Parker, Steve. *Eyewitness: Seashore*. New York: DK Publishing, 2000.

Rustad, Martha E. H., and Jody Rake. *Jellyfish*. Mankato, MN: Pebble Books, 2003.

Sharth, Sharon. *Sea Jellies: From Corals to Jellyfish*. Danbury, CT: Franklin Watts, 2002.

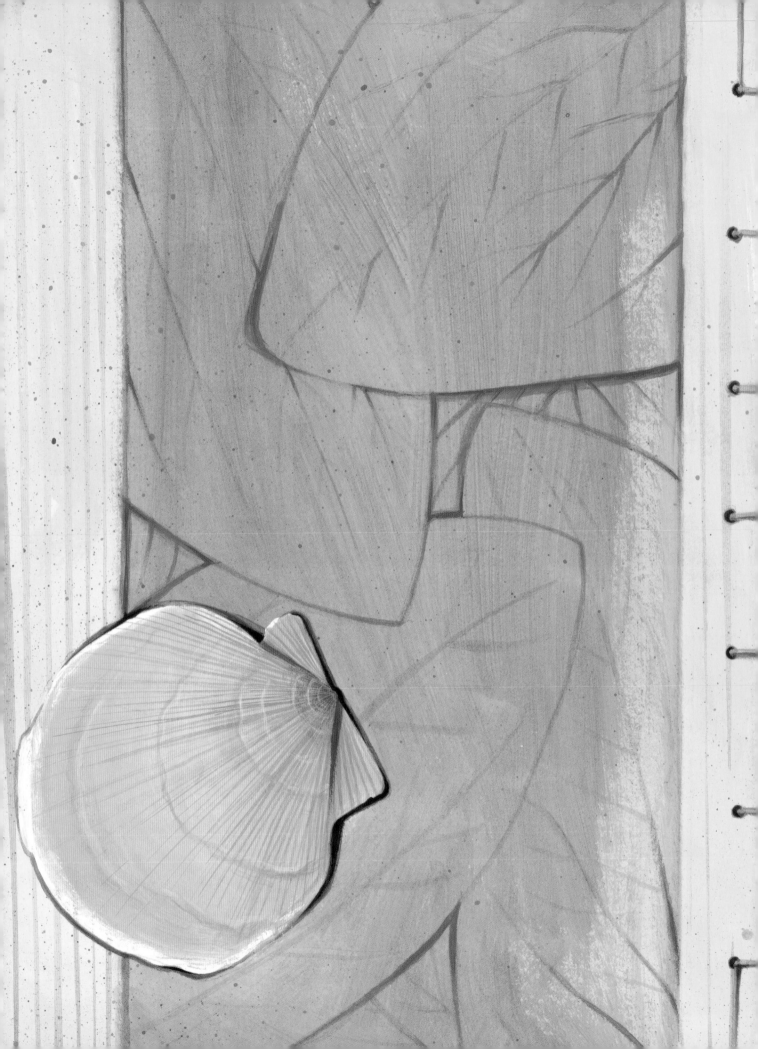